Swing Otto
Swing!

Swing Otto Swing!

story and pictures by
DAVID MILGRIM

Aladdin Paperbacks

New York London Toronto Sydney

ALADDIN PAPERBACKS
An imprint of Simon & Schuster Children's Publishing Division
1230 Avenue of the Americas, New York, NY 10020
ALADDIN PAPERBACKS, READY-TO-READ, and colophon are registered
trademarks of Simon & Schuster, Inc.
Also available in an Atheneum Books for Young Readers hardcover edition.
Designed by Sonia Chaghatzbanian
The text of this book was set in Century Old Style.
The illustrations were rendered in digital pen-and-ink.
Manufactured in the United States of America
First Aladdin Paperbacks edition October 2005

2 3 4 5 6 7 8 9 10
The Library of Congress has cataloged the hardcover edition as follows:
Milgrim, David.
Swing Otto swing / David Milgrim.—1st ed.
p. cm.
Summary: When Otto has trouble learning to swing on vines like his
monkey friends, he decides to make his own swing set instead.
ISBN-13: 978-0-689-85564-1 (hc.)
ISBN-10: 0-689-85564-8 (hc.)
[1. Monkeys—Fiction. 2. Swings—Fiction.] I. Title.
PZ7.M59485Sw   2004
[E]—dc21   2003001117
ISBN-13: 978-0-689-85565-8 (Aladdin pbk.)
ISBN-10: 0-689-85565-6 (Aladdin pbk.)

See Flip.

See Flip swing.

See Flop.

See Flop swing.

See Otto.

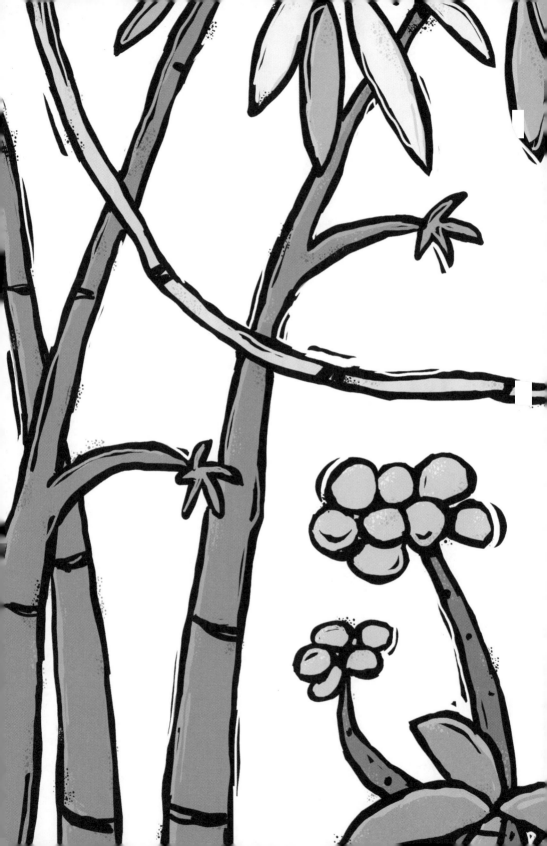

See Otto swing.

Hello, Otto.

Good-bye, Otto.

See Flip
give Otto
some tips.

See Otto try again.

See Flip and Flop
give Otto more tips.

See Otto learn.
Learn, Otto, learn.

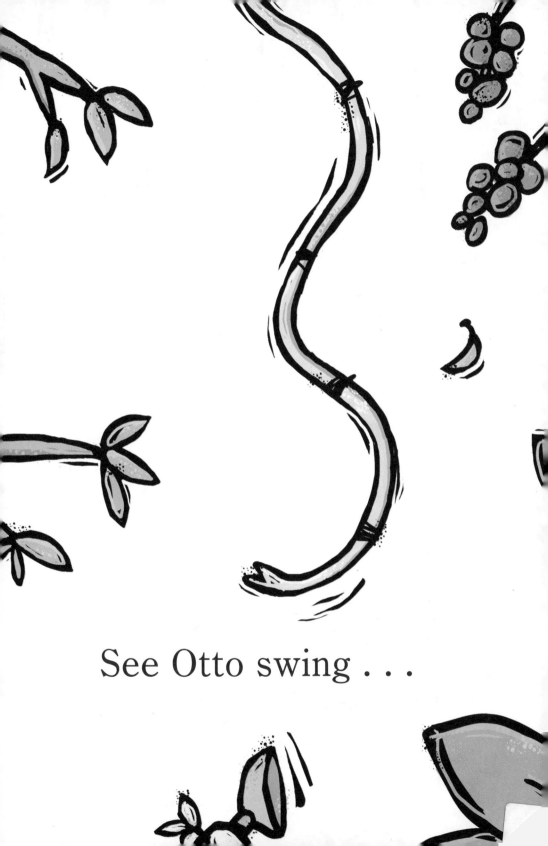

See Otto swing . . .

See Otto saw.
Saw, saw, saw.

See Otto tie.

Tie, tie, tie.

See Otto swing.
Swing, Otto, swing!